Lorenzo's Incredible Leap

A Story of Courage

Carol Schafer

Illustrated by
Alison Schafer Pahl

Carol Schafer

LORENZO'S INCREDIBLE LEAP: A STORY OF COURAGE

This is a work of fiction. Names, characters, places and incidents either are the product of the author's imagination or are used fictitiously, and any resemblance to actual persons, living or dead, businesses, companies, events, or locales is entirely coincidental.

Scripture taken from the New King James Version. Copyright © 1982 by Thomas Nelson, Inc. Used by permission. All rights reserved.

ISBN: 978-1-77069-608-2

Word Alive Press
131 Cordite Road, Winnipeg, MB R3W 1S1
www.wordalivepress.ca

WORD ALIVE PRESS
Just Write!

Library and Archives Canada Cataloguing in Publication
Schafer, Carol, 1956-
    Lorenzo's incredible leap : a story of courage / written by Carol Schafer ; illustrated by Alison Schafer Pahl.
ISBN 978-1-77069-608-2
    I. Pahl, Alison Schafer, 1988- II. Title.
PS8637.C41L67 2012   jC813'.6   C2012-903568-8

This book belongs to

_____

South
America

Peru
(Lorenzo lives
here)

Lorenzo wasn't sure he could do it. He looked this way and that way. He looked up and down. No matter how he looked at it, the dirt mound was way too big for him. He just knew it.

"Lorenzo," said his mother, "you are going to have to give it a try."

"I can't, Mom," said Lorenzo.

"You'll never know if you just keep standing there. Lorenzo, you'll never know all the things you can do in life if you just stand there and never try."

Lorenzo gulped hard. "But Mom, this mound is way too big. May I start with a smaller one? Please?"

Lorenzo's mother sighed softly. She was a patient mother llama, and she nearly always spoke kindly.

As for Lorenzo, he really did want to please his mother. *Maybe if I just take a little step I can get to the top,* he wondered to himself.

So he took a little step.

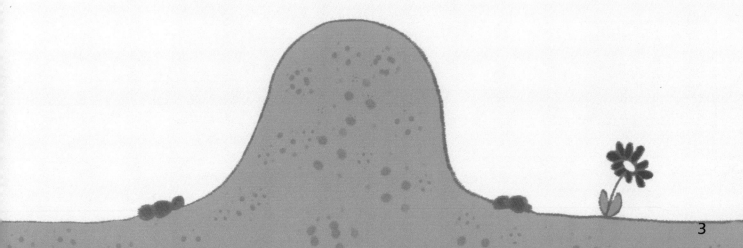

"That's a good start, Lorenzo," said Mother. "One step at a time—but one step alone won't get you very far."

Lorenzo thought hard. All the other llamas seemed happy to climb the big grassy mounds and stand on top of them. Sometimes they would sit. Sometimes they would line up and take turns standing and sitting on top of the big mounds. It looked like fun. Lorenzo thought about all the fun he could have standing and sitting on top of the mounds.

"Let's make a plan, Lorenzo," said his mother. He could tell that she had been thinking too. Maybe she had been thinking about this plan since yesterday. Or maybe even the day before.

"What kind of plan?" Lorenzo asked. He was curious what it might be.

"A daily plan."

"For every day?"

"Yes."

"For how long?"

"Until you can climb the dirt mound with confidence," Mother said.

Lorenzo gulped again. For a moment he was worried that he might have to follow this plan for the rest of his life. Or at least the rest of the summer.

"I'm ready," he said. And he tried to look positive.

"Here's how it will be, Lorenzo," said Mother.
"On Monday you will take one step up the dirt mound.
On Tuesday you will take two steps more than that.
On Wednesday you will take three steps more than Tuesday.
On Thursday you will take four steps more than Wednesday.
On Friday you will take five steps more than Thursday.
On Saturday you will take six steps more than Friday."
Lorenzo looked confused. That seemed like a lot of steps to him.
"What about on Sunday?" he asked.

mound = big   Wednesday

one step

3
+ 4
+ 5

Monday
+ Tuesday

Thursday

plan

spot   Friday

2 steps
+ 3 steps

so many steps

7

"We'll see," said Mother. "For now, you will start each day at this very same spot."

When Lorenzo woke up the next day it was Monday. He went with his mother to the spot. He took one step. That didn't seem so hard. In fact, it was easy.

"Now what do I do?" he asked.

"Nothing," said Mother. "Let's go home now."

All afternoon Lorenzo thought about the step he had taken. He wondered if Mother's plan would work after all.

The next morning he woke up and it was Tuesday. Lorenzo and his mother went to the spot.

"You need to take yesterday's step, and then two more," Mother said.

"Okay," Lorenzo said bravely.

Lorenzo finished in no time.

"Now what do I do?" he asked again.

"Nothing," Mother answered. "Let's go home."

All afternoon Lorenzo thought about how quickly he had finished taking his steps. In the way of llamas when they are curious, Lorenzo began to hum to himself as he wondered how things would go tomorrow.

The next morning when Lorenzo woke up it was already Wednesday.

"Let's go!" he said to Mother.

They got to the spot early. No other llamas were there yet. All the mounds were empty, except for one that Señor Lallo slept on when he sometimes fell asleep there after dark.

11

Lorenzo stood on the spot. Then he took one step for Monday. He took two steps for Tuesday. He took three steps for Wednesday. His legs felt stronger from all that exercise!

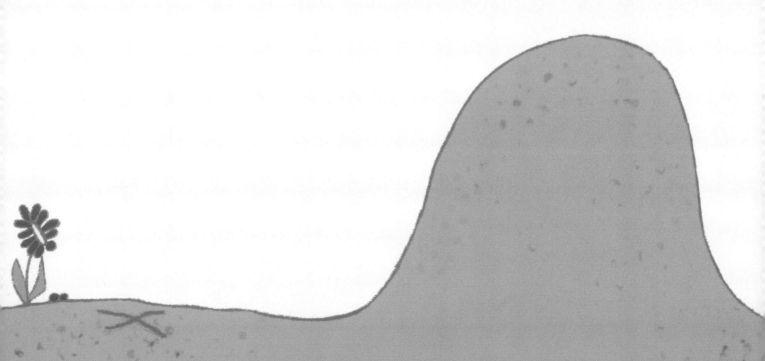

"Now what do I do?" Lorenzo asked his mother. He wondered if she would give the same answer as always.

"Nothing, Lorenzo. That's enough for today. Let's go home now."

All afternoon Lorenzo thought about the steps he had taken. He hadn't been afraid at all! He was so curious about tomorrow that he hummed most of the rest of the day.

When Lorenzo woke up the next morning it was Thursday. It was also raining. Lorenzo didn't feel like going anywhere!

"Time to go, Lorenzo," Mother called.

"But it's raining!" Lorenzo complained.

"What's a little rain to a young llama?" asked Mother.

Lorenzo could tell that she wasn't going to put up with any silliness. After all, they had agreed to a plan. Still, he thought he'd try one more time. He took another look. Sure enough, it was still raining.

"I'll get wet," he protested.

"I'll get cold," he fussed.

"I'll get smelly," he whined.

"LORENZO!"

Lorenzo took one look at his mother and skittered along. So—on Thursday Lorenzo and his mother went to the spot.

He took one step for Monday, and he sighed. He took two steps for Tuesday, and he whimpered. He took three steps for Wednesday, and he grumbled. He took four steps for Thursday, and he pouted.

Then, without even asking what to do next, Lorenzo turned around and walked home with his mother. He hung his head down. And, in the way of llamas when they are sad and anxious, he hummed a long, low hum all the way back.

The other llamas had all stayed in bed that morning because they knew the dirt mounds would really be more like mud mounds.

Lorenzo was muddy. He didn't like being wet and muddy and smelly. But in his heart he knew that he had done the right thing.

Lorenzo didn't know why it was so hard for him to do the things that other llamas found easy to do. But maybe if he stuck it out, no matter if the sun was shining or if it was raining, then maybe he could have more fun.

He hoped so.

The next morning when Lorenzo woke up it was Friday. The rain had stopped. He was glad about that. But instead of rain there was wind. Lorenzo hated the wind.

The wind got in his eyes and made them sting. The wind got in his ears and made them ring. The wind got in his hair and made it all tangled and twisted and messy. Lorenzo was angry!

17

Lorenzo went to his mother. "No way am I going out in this wind, Mother," he said.

Mother looked at her young llama. She frowned just a little bit, but she didn't say a word.

"The wind makes my eyes sting and my ears ring and my hair all tangled and twisted and messy."

"I see," said Mother. "Lorenzo," she said in a voice she only used on very serious occasions, "if you let small things stop you, how will you ever do any big things in your life?"

Lorenzo didn't have an answer.

Mother wasn't finished. She spoke again, using the same serious voice.

"Lorenzo, if you want to do all the normal things that llamas do—like standing and sitting on mounds—you are going to have to be bold enough to take the necessary steps.

"If you want to do interesting things in your life, then you will have to be strong enough to go out in the rain and take your steps on the muddy days as well as on the sunny days."

20

"And Lorenzo, if you want to do truly great things, you will have to be courageous enough to defy the wind and go out to take your steps even though your hair will get all tangled and twisted and messy.

"That's all there is to it," she said.
"Oh," said Lorenzo.

21

So out they went. It was true that Lorenzo's hair got tangled and twisted and messy. By the time they got to the spot Lorenzo was quite a sight! And so was his mother!

But Lorenzo took one step for Monday, then two more steps for Tuesday, then three steps for Wednesday, then four steps for Thursday, then five steps for Friday.

Then he looked back. He could hardly believe his eyes! What had happened?

Then he looked ahead. He could hardly believe his eyes again! What was happening?

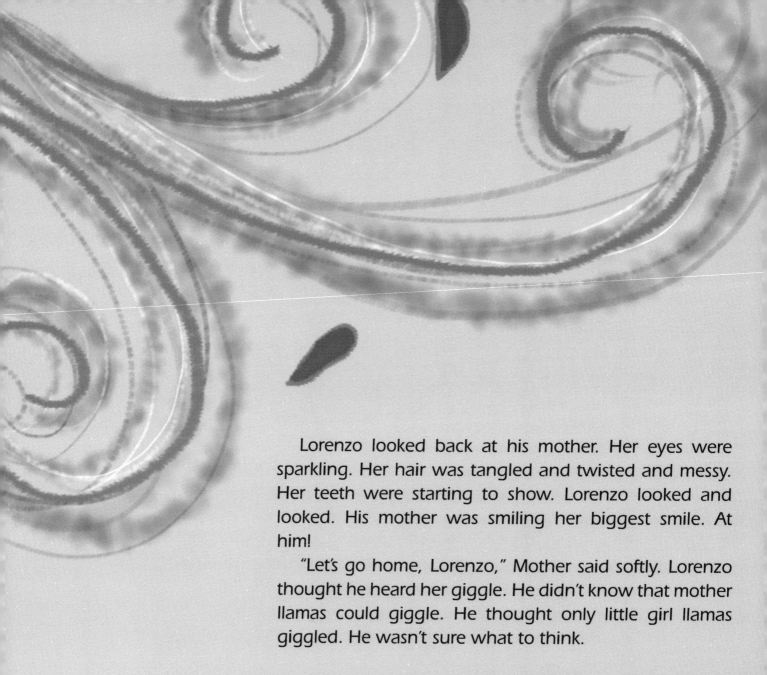

Lorenzo looked back at his mother. Her eyes were sparkling. Her hair was tangled and twisted and messy. Her teeth were starting to show. Lorenzo looked and looked. His mother was smiling her biggest smile. At him!

"Let's go home, Lorenzo," Mother said softly. Lorenzo thought he heard her giggle. He didn't know that mother llamas could giggle. He thought only little girl llamas giggled. He wasn't sure what to think.

That afternoon Lorenzo thought about a lot of things. Sunshine. Rain. Wind. Dirt mounds. Mud mounds. Llamas. Giggling. His mind was busy. He was so tired with all that thinking that he went to bed early.

The next morning when Lorenzo woke up it was Saturday. The sun was shining. It was not raining. It was not windy. But even if it had been raining or windy, Lorenzo wasn't afraid of those things anymore.

He was ready even before Mother called him. He wasn't sure, but she looked like she might have a secret that she couldn't talk about. Lorenzo was curious how the day would turn out. He hummed softly as he wondered. He wasn't afraid at all.

When Lorenzo and his mother got to the spot, Lorenzo was astonished to see all the other llamas gathered together.

He saw other young llamas lined up. He saw mother and father llamas lined up. Even grandma and grandpa llamas were lined up. But why?

"Lorenzo," said old Señor Lallo, "you have been bold and strong and courageous these past days. You have come out to take your steps in the rain and mud and wind. It seems like you are not as afraid of the dirt mound as you used to be. Your mother has helped you with a plan, and you have stuck to it! Now we have all come to see what happens next."

Lorenzo gulped a big gulp. He wasn't sure what would happen next. He wasn't sure what everyone had come to see. He wasn't sure he wanted anyone to watch him take his steps. But—oh well, if the rain hadn't stopped him, and the mud hadn't stopped him, and the wind hadn't stopped him, then perhaps it wouldn't be so awful if everyone was watching him.

Besides, it didn't look like they were going to leave.

So—Lorenzo was bold and strong and courageous. He took one step for Monday, then two steps for Tuesday, then three steps for Wednesday, then four steps for Thursday, then five steps for Friday, and six steps for Saturday. Lorenzo looked around. He could see the top of the mound!

And suddenly, to Lorenzo's great surprise, he took one step that was different from all the other steps.

Lorenzo took a big breath. And then he took a mighty leap. An enormous leap. An incredible leap that was unlike anything a llama could normally do.

Everyone looked up at Lorenzo. Everyone watched him go high in the air.

33

Then everyone watched him come down and land—right on top of the dirt mound!

"Hurray for Lorenzo!" someone yelled. And then everyone else started yelling and shouting and cheering for Lorenzo. They shouted and cheered until they had no voices left.

Lorenzo stretched his neck out and sniffed the excitement in the air. Then he twitched his ears to hear all the commotion.

35

"I knew you could do it, Lorenzo," Mother said. "One step at a time, no matter what." She nuzzled her son. And then, in the way of mother llamas when they are proud, she hummed into Lorenzo's ear. It felt good to him.

"I'm so proud of you," said Mother happily.

"Hey everyone, listen here," said Señor Lallo. "Lorenzo has been a good example for all of us. We need to celebrate his hard work and good success. After all, Lorenzo has shown us that we can all learn to be bold and strong and courageous.

"Now I have an excellent idea! We should all take a special vacation together!"

And so they did.

"Be strong and of good courage;
do not be afraid, nor be dismayed,
for the LORD your God is with you
wherever you go."
Joshua 1:9, NKJV

CPSIA information can be obtained
at www.ICGtesting.com
Printed in the USA
LVIW011152011012
300875LV00002B